Text and illustrations copyright © 2005 by Nick Bruel
A Neal Porter Book
Published by Roaring Brook Press
Roaring Brook Press is a division of Holtzbrinck
Publishing Holdings Limited Partnership
143 West Street, New Milford, Connecticut 06776

Distributed in Canada by H. B. Fenn and Company Ltd.

Library of Congress Cataloging-in-
Publication Data
Bruel, Nick.
Bad kitty / Nick Bruel.—1st ed.
p. cm.
Summary: When a kitty discovers
there is no cat food in the house, she
decides to become very, very bad.
ISBN 1-59643-069-9
[1. Cats—Fiction.   2. Food—Fiction.
3. Behavior—Fiction.   4. Alphabet.]
I. Title.
PZ7.B82832Bad 2005
[E]—dc22
2004024456

FOR CARINA

Roaring Brook Press books are
available for special promotions
and premiums.
For details contact: Director of
Special Markets, Holtzbrinck Publishers

First edition October 2005
Printed in Mexico
10   9   8   7   6

She
wasn't
always
a
bad
kitty.

She used to be a good kitty,

until one day . . .

OH, DEAR!
WE'RE ALL OUT OF
FOOD FOR THE KITTY! ⟍
ALL WE HAVE ARE
SOME HEALTHY
AND DELICIOUS ...

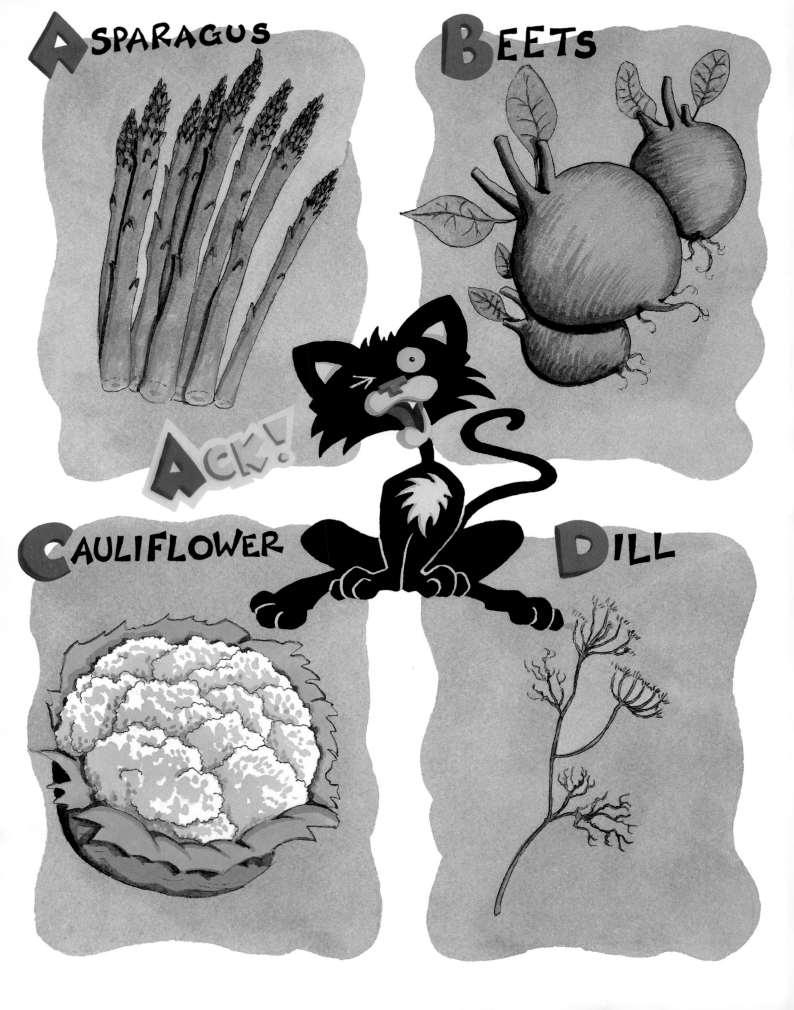

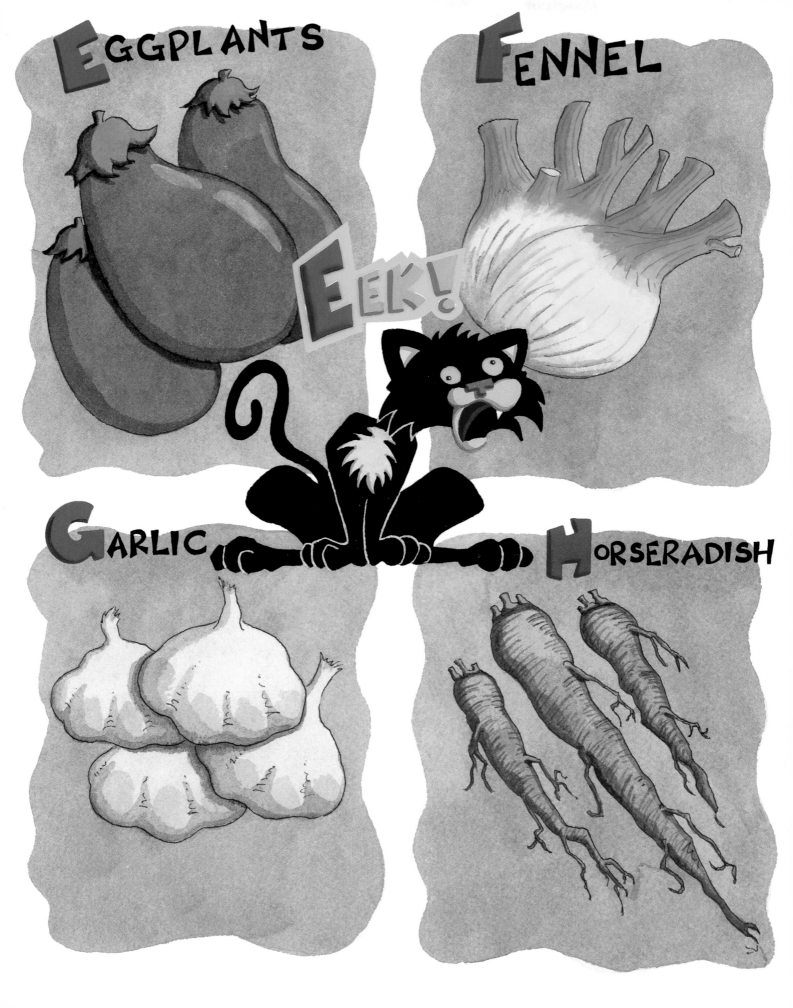

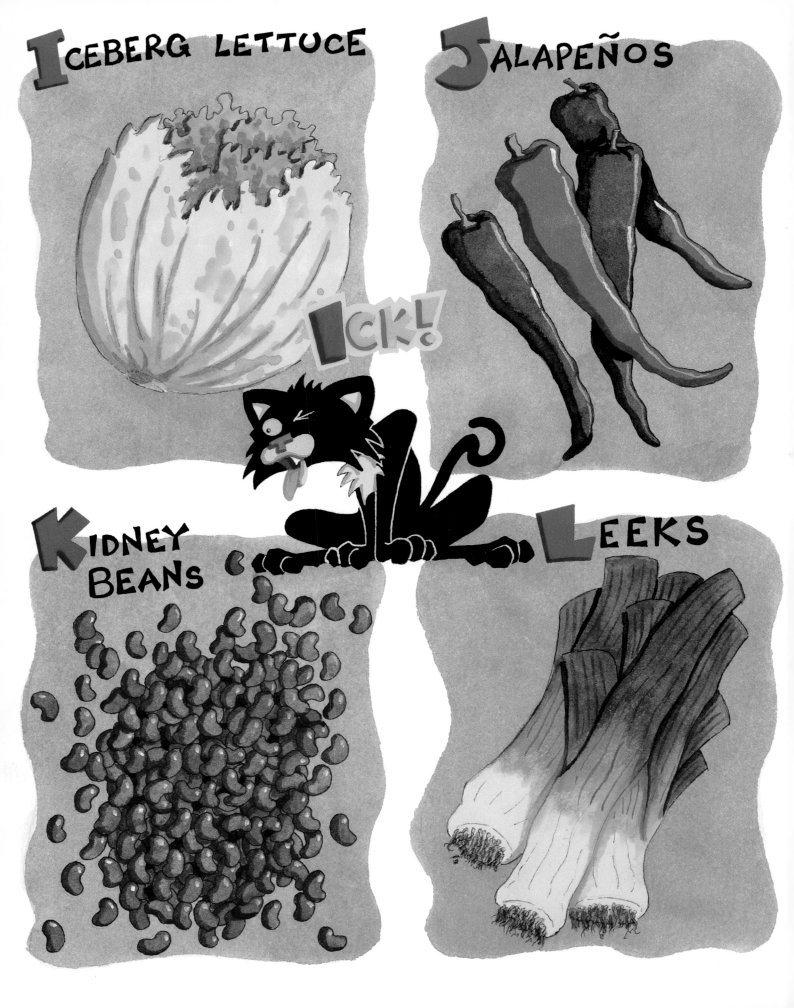

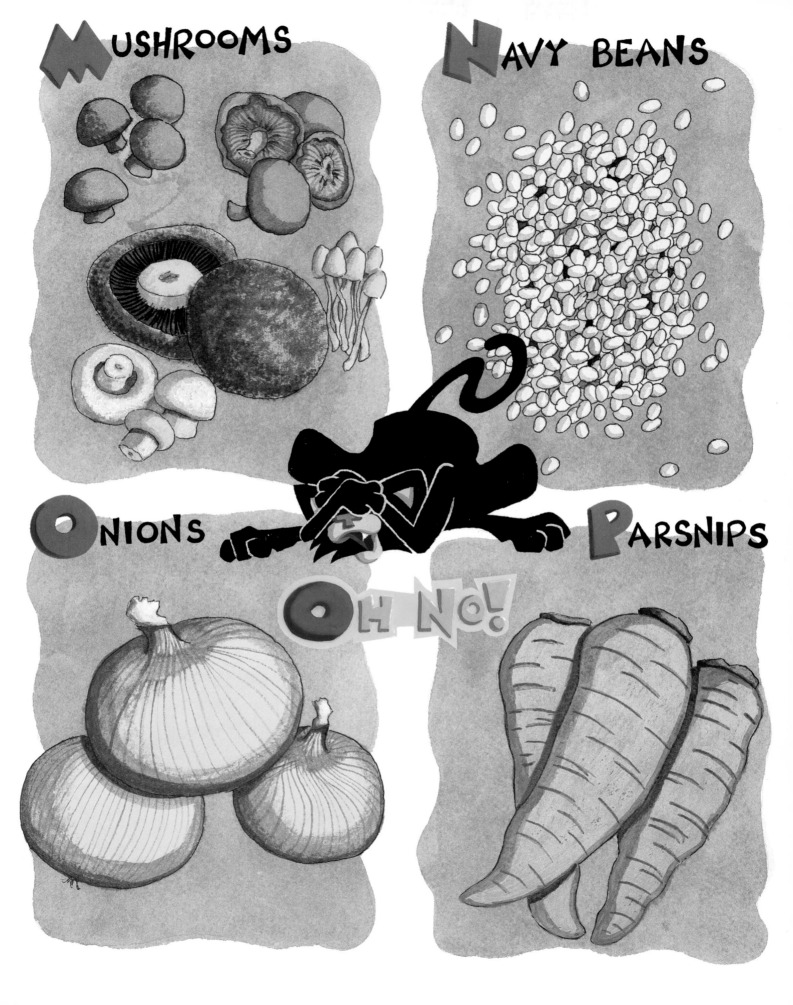

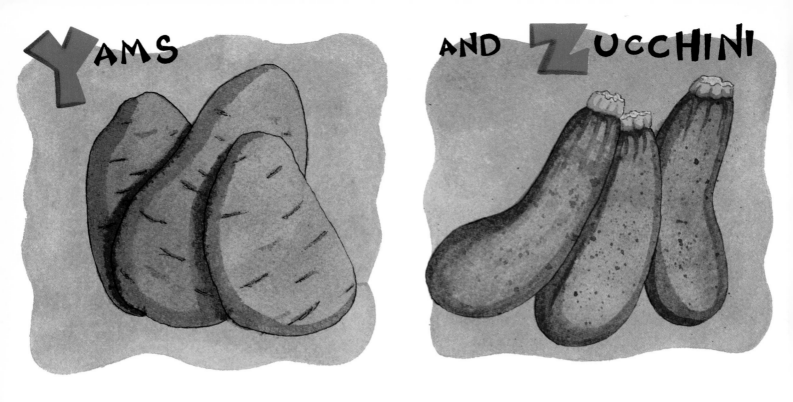

Yams and Zucchini

Kitty was not happy.
Not happy at all.

That's when she decided
she would be a
BAD kitty.

But not just any bad
kitty—a very, very, bad,
bad, BAD kitty.

She . . .

ATE MY HOMEWORK

BIT GRANDMA

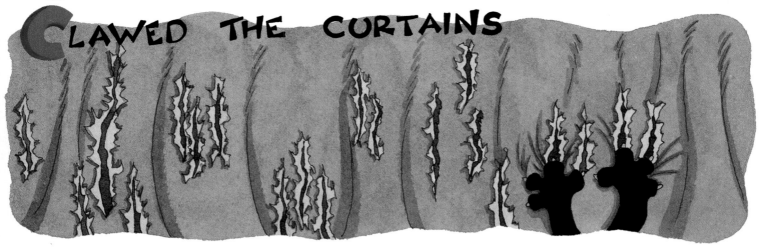

CLAWED THE CURTAINS

DAMAGED THE DISHES

ENDANGERED THE GOLDFISH

FLOODED THE BATHROOM

GRAPPLED WITH GUESTS

HURLED HAIR BALLS AT OUR HEADS

WAS MEAN TO MY MOMMY

WAS NASTY TO DADDY'S NECKTIES

OVERTURNED HER CAT BOX

PLOTTED AGAINST US

Quarreled with our Neighbor

Ruined the Rug

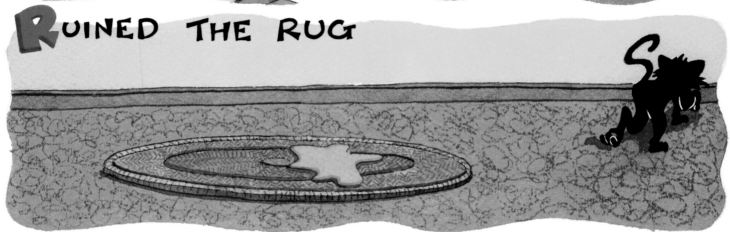

Sold My Toys

Tormented a Little Mouse

UNTIED MY SHOES

WAS VIOLENT WITH THE VET

WROTE ON THE WALLS

EXAMINED MY DIARY

What a bad kitty.

What a very, very, bad, bad, bad kitty.

But then . . .

I'M BACK FROM
THE GROCERY STORE!
LOOK AT ALL THE
GOOD FOOD I BOUGHT
FOR KITTY!

WE HAVE . . .

YAK YOGURT   AND BAKED ZEBRA ZITI

Now, kitty was happy!
Very, very happy!

She decided that from now on, she would be a GOOD kitty!

But not just any good kitty—a very, very, good, good, good, kitty!

She . . .

INVITED AFFECTION

JOINED THE JAMBOREE

KISSED THE GOLDFISH

LEFT THE LAMP ALONE

MOPPED THE BATHROOM

WAS **N**ICE TO MY MOMMY

SANG **O**PERA ALL NIGHT

BRAVO!
ENCORE!
MORE!
MORE!

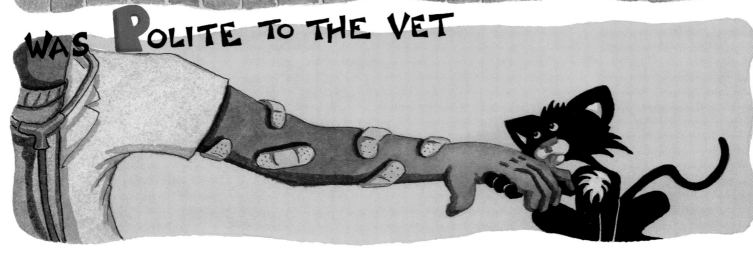

WAS **P**OLITE TO THE VET

QUIT QUARRELING WITH OUR NEIGHBOR

REPAIRED THE CURTAINS

SAVED THE DAY

TIED MY SHOES

DIDN'T EAT UNCLE MURRAY

WHEW!

VACUUMED THE FLOOR

WASHED THE CAR

FILED OUR TAXES

What a good kitty!

What a very, very
good, good, good kitty!

How can we reward such a good kitty?

I know . . .

LOOK, KITTY! WE'VE BROUGHT YOU A NEW FRIEND! YOU CAN PLAY TOGETHER, AND YOU CAN GO TO THE PARK TOGETHER, AND YOU CAN SHARE YOUR FOOD WITH HIM!

Uh-oh . . .